SIMON & SCHUSTER BOOKS FOR YOUNG READERS · An imprint of Simon & Schuster Children's Publishing Division · 1230 Avenue of the Americas, New York, New York 10020 · Copyright © 2011 by Emily Gravett First published in Great Britain in 2011 by Macmillan Children's Books, London. · First U.S. edition 2012 · All rights reserved, including the right of reproduction in whole or in part in any form. SIMON & SCHUSTER BOOKS FOR YOUNG READERS is a trademark of Simon & Schuster, Inc. · For information about special discounts for bulk purchases, please contact · Simon & Schuster Special Sales at 1-866-506-1949 or business@simonandschuster.com. The Simon & Schuster Speakers Bureau can bring authors to your live event. · For more information or to book an event, contact the Simon & Schuster Speakers Bureau at 1-866-248-3049 or visit our website at www.simonspeakers.com. · The text for this book is handlettered. · The illustrations for this book are rendered in watercolor and oil based pencil. · Manufactured in China · 0411 MCM · 10 9 8 7 6 5 4 3 2 1 Library of Congress Cataloging-in-Publication Data · Gravett, Emily. · Wolf won't bite! / Emily Gravett.—1st U.S. ed. · p. cm. · Summary: Three little circus pigs capture a wild wolf and make him do outrageous tricks, safe in the belief that he would never bite them. · ISBN 978-1-4424-2763-1 (hardcover) · [1. Pigs—Fiction. 2. Wolves—Fiction. 3. Circus—Fiction.] I. Title. II. Title: Wolf will not bite! · PZ7.G77577Wo 2012 · [E]—dc22 · 2011000773

For Maureen and John

We have caught a WILD WOLF!

I can stand him on a stool!

I can dress him in a bow...

I can ride him like a horse but WOLF WON'T BITE!

I can make
him jump

through hoops!

I can make
him dance
a jig but...

through the air!

We can even
place our heads

between his

mighty

jaws

but WOLF WON'T...